South Pole Penguins

Adventures of Riley™
South Pole Penguins

BY
Amanda Lumry
AND
Laura Hurwitz

Dear Riley,
How would you like to join me, Aunt Martha, and Cousin Alice at the bottom of the world?
We're going to Antarctica, the coldest place on Earth, to study penguins and what they eat! Rising temperatures are changing the Antarctic food web, and even small changes can have big effects on the animal population.
Be sure to pack your boots and nose plugs! See you in November. . . .
Uncle Max

SCHOLASTIC PRESS ★ NEW YORK

A special thank-you to all the scientists who collaborated on this project. Your time and assistance are very much appreciated.

First published in China in 2007 by Eaglemont Press.
www.eaglemont.com

All photographs by Amanda Lumry except:
Page 22 and page 32 emperor penguins with chick © Konrad Wothe/Getty Images
Pages 22–23 emperor penguin colony © David Tipling/Getty Images
Pages 24–25 emperor penguin colony © Art Wolfe/Getty Images

Illustrations and Layouts by Ulkutay & Ulkutay, London WC2E 9RZ
Editing and Digital Compositing by Michael E. Penman
Digital Imaging by Phoenix Color

Library of Congress Control Number: 2006024465

ISBN-13: 978-0-545-06835-2
ISBN-10: 0-545-06835-5

10 9 8 7 6 5 4 3 2 1   08 09 10 11 12

Printed in Mexico   49
First Scholastic printing, November 2008

A portion of the proceeds from your purchase of this licensed product supports the stated educational mission of the Smithsonian Institution— "the increase and diffusion of knowledge." The name of the Smithsonian Institution and the sunburst logo are registered trademarks of the Smithsonian Institution and are registered in the U.S. Patent and Trademark Office. www.si.edu

2% of the proceeds from this book will be donated to the Wildlife Conservation Society. http://wcs.org

An average royalty of approximately 3 cents from the sale of each book in the Adventures of Riley series will be received by World Wildlife Fund (WWF) to support their international efforts to protect endangered species and their habitats. ® WWF Registered Trademark Panda Symbol © 1986 WWF. © 1986 Panda symbol WWF-World Wide Fund For Nature (also known as World Wildlife Fund) ® "WWF" is a WWF Registered Trademark © 1986 WWF-Fonds Mondial pour la Nature symbole du panda Marque Déposée du WWF ®
www.worldwildlife.org

A portion of the proceeds from your purchase of this product supports The Wyland Foundation, a 501(c)(3) nonprofit organization founded in 1993 by environmental marine life artist Wyland. By bridging the worlds of art and science, the Wyland Foundation strives to inspire people of all ages to become better stewards of our oceans and global water resources.
http://wylandfoundation.org
www.wyland.com

We try to produce the most beautiful books possible and we are extremely concerned about the impact of our manufacturing process on the forests of the world and the environment as a whole. Accordingly, we made sure that the paper used in this book has been certified as coming from forests that are managed to ensure the protection of the people and wildlife dependent upon them.

"Winners get the fort!"
Riley yelled. He and his friend Maria
threw snowballs at the other team, then
ducked behind their little snow fort.
Splat! A big snowball hit Riley's cheek.

"Gotcha," yelled Riley's friend Mike.

"When you get back from
Antarctica, we'll build a giant snow
fort so that no one can beat us,"
said Maria.

"I can't wait," said Riley.

1

Soon it was time for Riley to make the long trip south. He met up with Uncle Max, Aunt Martha, and Cousin Alice in Ushuaia, Argentina.

"This ship will be our home base for the next week," said Uncle Max. "To reach Antarctica, we'll have to cross the **dreaded** Drake Passage. It has some of the roughest seas in the world."

"Can't we go a different way?" asked Riley.

"I hope not," said Alice. "Think of the waves and the wind. It'll be fun!"

NORTH POLE

The Drake Passage

Antarctica   Ushuaia

SOUTH POLE

That night, Riley wore his nose plugs to dinner.

"Do we smell that bad?" joked Alice.

"I wasn't sure what they were for," said Riley, turning red.

"We'll be collecting stinky guano in Antarctica, and nose plugs will help block the smell," said Uncle Max.

"Gwa-no?" asked Riley.

"Penguin poop!" said Alice.

"I'll be looking under the microscope for traces of krill in the penguin guano," said Uncle Max. "Krill are small **crustaceans** that look a lot like the shrimp on your plate. They are a major food source for penguins and an important part of the Antarctic food web."

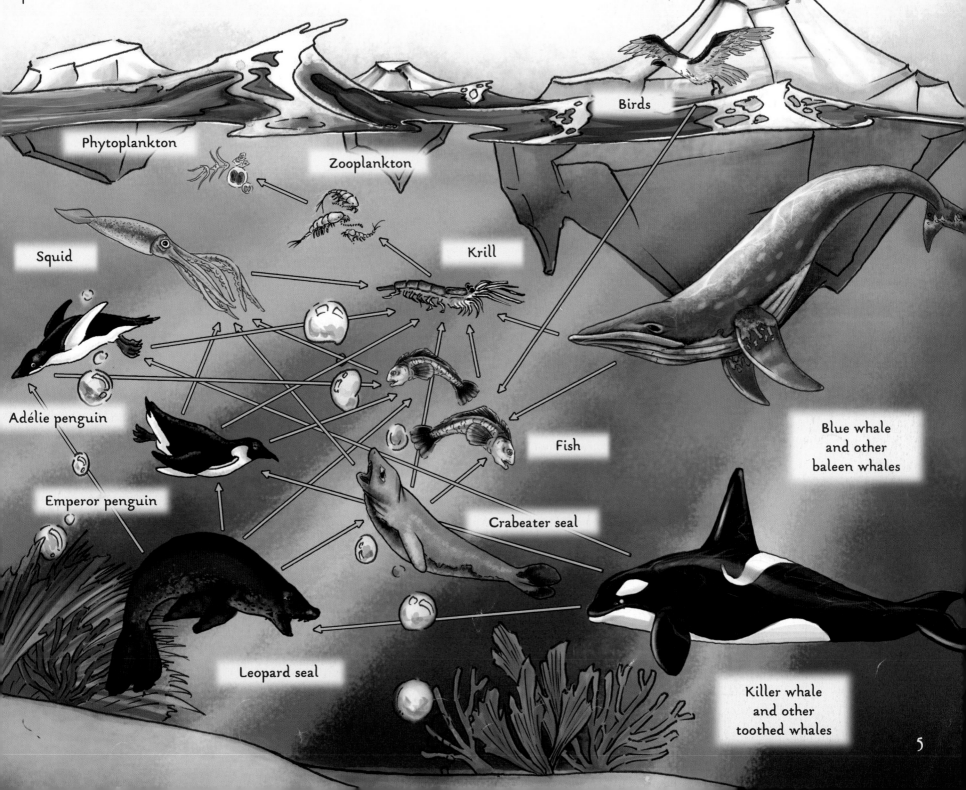

Birds

Phytoplankton

Zooplankton

Squid

Krill

Adélie penguin

Fish

Blue whale and other baleen whales

Emperor penguin

Crabeater seal

Leopard seal

Killer whale and other toothed whales

Cape Petrel

▶ This bird will defend its nesting place by spitting stomach oil at intruders.

▶ Its main food source is krill.

▶ Though it lives in Antarctica, it may fly as far as the Galápagos Islands to find food.

—Maxwell "Uncle Max" Plimpton, Professor and Senior Field Biologist

Southern Ocean

▶ In 2000, the Antarctic Ocean was renamed the Southern Ocean.

▶ Every winter much of the Southern Ocean freezes, which almost doubles the size of Antarctica.

▶ The Southern Ocean is the world's fourth-largest ocean.

—Wyland, Artist and Naturalist

For the next two days, the ship rocked and rolled through the Drake Passage. All around them, the Pacific and Atlantic Oceans crashed together with a mighty force. The swirling winds took Alice's breath away, but the view was worth it. What a great way to start their adventure!

On the third morning, the seas calmed. They had survived the "Drake Shake"!

All of a sudden, both Riley and Alice yelled...

"LAND!"

"I saw it first!" Alice shouted.

"No, you didn't!" Riley shouted back. "We saw it at the same time."

"You two sound like the first visitors to Antarctica," said Aunt Martha. "Everyone who came here wanted to claim it. That's why, in 1961, the Antarctic Treaty was created to preserve Antarctica as a research location, owned by no one, and belonging to all."

"So now, instead of competing against one another, nations can work together to help protect this **majestic** land," added Uncle Max. "Especially as climate change continues to melt the Antarctic ice and affect the food web."

Crabeater Seal

➤ People misnamed it, thinking it ate crabs because its dung was pink. It actually eats krill.

➤ It can eat 20 to 25 times its body weight in a year.

—Dee Allen, Marine Mammal Museum Specialist, National Museum of Natural History, Smithsonian Institution

"Why is the water pink?" asked Riley.

"That's a **swarm** of krill," said Uncle Max. "In recent years, the world's krill population has shrunk by 80 percent. Phytoplankton, the tiny plants floating on the ocean's surface, which are the main food source for krill, have been dying off as well."

"Is there enough krill left for the penguins to eat?" asked Riley.

"No. Right now, krill and penguins are both in trouble," said Uncle Max. "The problem is that the world's air pollution is acting like a blanket and warming the planet, including the oceans. Warmer temperatures and changes in the food web make it hard for krill, and phytoplankton, to survive."

"Here's what krill look like up close," said Uncle Max.

Antarctic Krill

- ➤ It is almost as long as a crayon and weighs only .007 lb. (3 g).
- ➤ It lives up to 6 years.
- ➤ It is the main food source for Antarctic wildlife.
- ➤ It lives in large groups in the ocean (a billion or more members).

—Dr. Rafael Lemaitre, Chair and Curator/ Research Biologist, Department of Invertebrate Zoology, National Museum of Natural History, Smithsonian Institution

KRILL DIAGRAM

antennae

compound eyes

gastric mill

hepatopancreas

ice rakes

gills

gut

swimming legs

As the ship got closer to land, Riley and Alice could see a **colony** of Adélie penguins nesting on the bank.

"This is our first stop," said Uncle Max. "Be sure to rinse your boots in the bucket before leaving the ship!"

"Why do we have to clean our boots?" asked Alice.

"We don't want to bring anything into Antarctica, such as dirt or germs, that wasn't already there," said Aunt Martha.

They climbed into the dinghy, where they had a front-row seat to the bottom of the world.

"Brrr," said Alice. "It's colder than I expected."

"This is exactly what I thought Antarctica would be like," said Riley. "But better!"

On shore, Riley helped Uncle Max take water and guano samples. Alice tried not to step in the guano, but it was no use. Within seconds, her boots were covered in pink goo.

"I had to wash my boots for *this*?" Alice asked.

Minke Whale

➤ Its Latin name means "sharp nose."

➤ It is the smallest of the whales—around 33 ft. (10 m) long, about the same length as an orca.

—Karen Baragona, Leader, Whale and Dolphin Conservation Program, World Wildlife Fund

Elephant Seal

➤ Its huge nose looks like an elephant's trunk, which it **inflates** while roaring at enemies.

➤ It can dive up to 2,000 ft. (600 m) deep and hold its breath for more than 20 minutes.

—Claudio Campagna, Researcher and Associate Conservation Zoologist, Wildlife Conservation Society

"Remember, dear," said Uncle Max. "Guano tells me a lot about a penguin's diet. Besides, pink guano is a good thing. It means that these penguins are getting enough krill to eat."

15

That night, Riley dreamed of being the first explorer to Antarctica.

By morning, they had reached Iceberg Alley, an area near the Antarctic **Peninsula**. The ship was surrounded by a sea of ice! Some chunks were the size of regular ice cubes, while others were huge icebergs the size of city blocks.

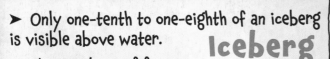

Iceberg

➤ Only one-tenth to one-eighth of an iceberg is visible above water.

➤ It is made up of frozen freshwater, not salt water.

➤ An iceberg the size of a small house is called a bergy bit.

—Linda Welzenback, Meteorite Collections Manager, National Museum of Natural History, Smithsonian Institution

"Today is our once-in-a-lifetime chance to study the famous emperor penguins of Snow Hill Island!" said Uncle Max. "The samples I collect there will help prove that the penguins' diets have changed now that there is less krill for them to eat. The only way to reach this **colony** is by helicopter."

Southern Giant Petrel

➤ It can fly more than 300 miles (500 km) in one day.

➤ A male petrel will feed mainly along the coast, while a female will feed mainly over the ocean.

—Dr. Flavio Quintana, Associate Researcher, Wildlife Conservation Society

19

From the air they saw a long line of penguins stretching back as far as the eye could see.

"It looks like a conveyor belt of penguins," said Riley.

"Do they ever stop to rest?" asked Alice.

"They can't," said Uncle Max. "Emperor penguins have to make the most of every moment and work together in order to survive. Every winter, each female lays just one egg. The male must **incubate** it within the safety of the **colony**, while the female travels more than twenty-five miles to the sea to get food."

"That's one long walk!" said Riley.

"Their journey can take several weeks, but some penguin **colonies** have to travel more than twice that distance," Uncle Max told him. "When the female returns, she **regurgitates** the food for the newly hatched chick to eat, while the male makes the same trip to the ocean to feed."

21

They landed a safe distance away from the large, and loud, emperor penguin **colony.** There were mothers, fathers, and chicks everywhere, trumpeting and singing loudly while sunning, feeding, and just waddling around. As Uncle Max and Aunt Martha unloaded the helicopter, Riley and Alice ran out to take pictures.

Emperor Penguin

➤ It is the largest of all the penguins.

➤ It can dive up to 1,750 ft. (530 m) deep and hold its breath for 20 minutes.

➤ Instead of walking, sometimes it will **toboggan** on its belly across the snow and ice!

—Dr. Taylor Ricketts, Director, Conservation Science, World Wildlife Fund

Suddenly, a gust of wind blew Alice's hat high into the air. Riley raced to catch it, but it sailed out of reach. Alice saw her parents waving and shouting. A storm was coming!

"That's the emergency signal," said Alice. "We have to go!"
Riley jumped for the hat one last time—and got it! He stuffed it into his backpack and then raced Alice back to the helicopter.

25

With the freezing wind in their faces, the race was more like a crawl.
"What about your dad's samples?" Riley yelled.

"If we don't take off right away, we could be stuck here for good!" said Alice.
No one had time to do anything but reload the helicopter and fly back to the safety of the ship.

"The weather here changes quickly," said Aunt Martha. "Those **katabatic winds** can come out of nowhere and are very dangerous. I hope we got everything!"

"We got everything except what I came here for, my guano sample," said a glum Uncle Max.

"And once again, my boots are covered in goo," said Alice.

"Wait," said Riley. "Uncle Max, look! Alice is wearing your sample. Fresh guano!"

"Great thinking, Riley!" said Uncle Max. "Let's go up top for a better look."

Upper Decks

Cabins

"Here's my boot goop!" said Alice.

"Thanks!" said Riley. He filled a test tube and handed it to Uncle Max. "Why is this guano green and not pink?"

"The emperor penguins are eating algae as a last resort, since they can't find any krill or fish," said Uncle Max. "The algae turns their poop green and isn't very healthy for them. This shows that the Antarctic food chain is in real danger."

"Riley's sharp eyes and Alice's boots gave us the information we needed," said Aunt Martha. "As the Antarctic Treaty and emperor penguins taught us, you can accomplish a lot more when you work together."

That gives me an idea, thought Riley. The ship turned around and began the long voyage home.

When he got back, Riley gave Maria a picture of an emperor penguin family. Instead of building a big snow fort, Riley, Maria, and Mike built a huge snow penguin for everyone in the neighborhood to enjoy together.

Riley returned to living the life of a nine-year-old, until the next letter arrived from Uncle Max....

Where will Riley go next?

FURTHER INFORMATION

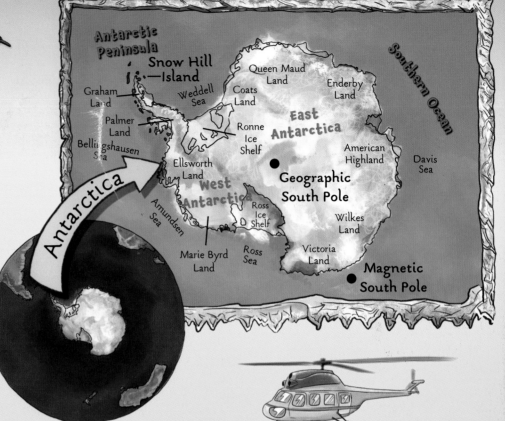

Glossary

colony: a group of the same animals living together

crustaceans: animals such as crabs and lobsters that live in the water, breathe through gills, have a hard outer covering, and have jointed arms and legs

Wyland is a world-renowned artist, adventurer, and advocate for our blue planet. His adventurous spirit has led him across the globe to photograph, sculpt, and paint amazing marine life. Through his art, Wyland inspires others to take care of our precious water habitats. He is on a mission to paint 100 giant murals around the world to share the beauty of art and his passion for the ocean. His largest mural, in Destin, Florida, covers more than seven acres and is larger than his previous mural in the Guinness Book of World Records!

In 1993, Wyland started the Wyland Foundation, a group dedicated to raising awareness about the world's oceans, waterways, and marine life. With the Wyland Foundation, Wyland spends much of his time traveling around the world, educating kids and their families about the importance of clean water and how they can make healthy choices for a healthy environment.

dreaded: thought about with fear

incubate: to sit on eggs and keep them warm so they will hatch

inflate: to make something expand by filling it with air

katabatic winds: cold winds that blow in a downward direction and increase speed rapidly

majestic: very beautiful

peninsula: land surrounded by water on three sides

regurgitate: to bring partly digested food from the stomach into the mouth

swarm: a large crowd of living things

toboggan: to slide or coast

JOIN US FOR MORE GREAT ADVENTURES!

RILEY'S WORLD

Visit our Web site at

www.adventuresofriley.com

to find out how
you can join Riley's
super kids' club!

ADVENTURES OF RILEY™

**Look for these other
great Riley books:**

➤ Safari in South Africa

➤ Project Panda

➤ Polar Bear Puzzle